For Jata - D.B.

For Eve - C.B.S.

GRANDFATHER'S WHEELYTHING

by Duncan Ball

illustrated by
Cat Bowman Smith

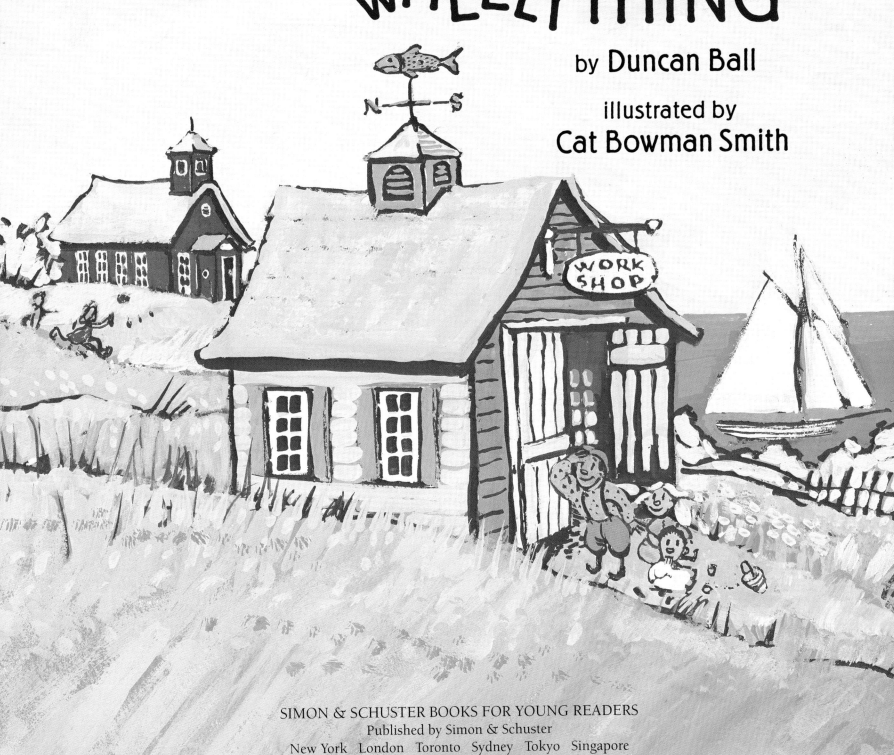

SIMON & SCHUSTER BOOKS FOR YOUNG READERS
Published by Simon & Schuster
New York London Toronto Sydney Tokyo Singapore

Grandfather's wheelything went up

and went down.

It raced and it raced

through the streets of our town.

Everyone loved it. It was such a delight

when he wheeled it in daytime

and he wheeled it at night.

He wheeled it in snowstorms

and he wheeled it in rain.

He wheeled it and wheeled it,
and he wheeled it again.

Faster and faster he rose and he dropped.

Nothing could slow him,

so he suddenly

stopped.

SIMON & SCHUSTER BOOKS FOR YOUNG READERS
Simon & Schuster Building, Rockefeller Center, 1230 Avenue of the Americas, New York, New York 10020. Text copyright © 1994 by Duncan Ball. Illustrations copyright © 1994 by Cat Bowman Smith. All rights reserved including the right of reproduction in whole or in part in any form. SIMON & SCHUSTER BOOKS FOR YOUNG READERS is a trademark of Simon & Schuster. Designed by David Neuhaus. The text for this book is set in Berkeley Old Style. The illustrations were done in gouache. Manufactured in the United States of America.   10 9 8 7 6 5 4 3 2 1

Library of Congress Cataloging-in-Publication Data: Ball, Duncan. Grandfather's wheelything / by Duncan Ball; illustrated by Cat Bowman Smith. Summary: Grandfather's wheelything races around the town in all kinds of weather, delighting those who see it. [1. Vehicles—Fiction.   2. Grandfathers—Fiction.   3. Stories in rhyme.] I. Smith, Cat Bowman, ill.   II. Title.   PZ8.3.B2015Gr 1994 [E]—dc20 93-12524 CIP ISBN: 0-671-79817-0